GRACIE
La Roo
IN THE SNOW
written by MARSHA QUA
illustrated by KRISTYNA LI
raintree
a Capstone company — publishers for children
D0755409
C334413670

Raintree is an imprint of Capstone Global Library Limited, a company incorporated in England and Wales having its registered office at 264 Banbury Road, Oxford, OX2 7DY – Registered company number: 6695582

www.raintree.co.uk
myorders@raintree.co.uk

Designed by Hilary Wacholz
Original illustrations © Capstone Global Library Limited 2019
Originated by Capstone Global Library Ltd
Printed and bound in India

ISBN 978 1 4747 7011 8
22 21 20 19 18
10 9 8 7 6 5 4 3 2 1

British Library Cataloguing in Publication Data
A full catalogue record for this book is available from the British Library.

CONTENTS

GRACIE and The

NAME: Gracie LaRoo

TEAM: Water Sprites

CLAIM TO FAME:
Being the youngest pig to join a world-renowned synchronized swimming team!

SIGNATURE MOVE:
"When Pigs Fly" Spin

LIKES: Purple, clip-on tail bows, mud baths, newly mown hay smell

DISLIKES: Too much attention, doing laundry, scary films

QUOTE

"I just hope I can be the kind of synchronized swimmer my team needs!"

WATER SPRITES
JINI
BARB
JIA
SU
MARTHA
BRADY
SILVIA

GRACIE'S DREAM

The Sprites had a special performance at a posh ski resort. When they had finished, they headed to the changing room.

"What's everyone doing later?" Silvia asked.

All of the Sprites answered quickly: Sleeping. Reading. Mending costumes.

"I am going to learn to ski," Gracie said.

The Sprites all started talking at the same time.

"Are you crazy?"

"You'll get hurt!"

"You're joking!"

"I went to the ski school this morning. I've booked a lesson for after the show," Gracie said.

"I'm going to come and watch," said Jini.

"You don't have to," Gracie said. "I'm sure you are busy."

"Nonsense. We are all going to come," Silvia said. "Right, Sprites?"

"Yay!" they yelled.

Gracie didn't know what to say. She was the best swimmer on the team. But she didn't know how to ski. Gracie didn't want her friends to see her fail.

CHAPTER 2

GRACIE SKIS!

The Sprites were on the balcony waiting for Gracie's skiing lesson to begin. They cheered when she walked out with her teacher, Kezzie.

Kezzie showed Gracie how to put on the skis. It was much harder than Gracie thought it would be.

SKI LESSON
MEETING POINT

"Get used to how they feel. Try to hop and shuffle," Kezzie said.

Hopping was tricky. The heavy boots and skis didn't want to move. Shuffling was easy. Gracie moved her skis back and forth and side to side.

The Sprites cheered from the balcony. "Well done, Gracie!"

Gracie felt embarrassed.

"When you want to stop or slow down, make a V with your skis. That's called a snowplough. Now you try," Kezzie said.

Kezzie pushed her skis until the tips came together. The backs were far apart. It looked like she was making an upside-down V.

Gracie pushed her skis, but they didn't make the letter V. They just kept getting wider apart. Her legs were stretched so far she couldn't go up or down. She couldn't move at all!

The Sprites laughed, but Kezzie turned to them and glared. She lifted Gracie and put her in place.

"Try again," Kezzie said. "You can do it."

This time Gracie made a perfect V.

Kezzie showed Gracie how to climb up a small hill, step by step.

"Good work! Now you are going to ski back down the small hill," Kezzie said.

"I am?" Gracie asked.

"Yes, you are," Kezzie said. "Just focus on what I taught you."

Gracie shuffled her skis until she was facing downhill. Before she knew it, she was skiing!

CHAPTER 3

FALLING AGAIN

Down, down, down. Faster, faster, faster.

"Snowplough!" Kezzie cried.

Gracie pushed her boots until the tips of her skis came together. She slowed down.

"I did it!" she shouted.

She turned to look at Kezzie, and before she knew it she was tumbling into the snow.

Gracie could hear her friends laughing.

Kezzie swooshed to her side.

"Are you okay?" she asked.

Gracie said, "I'm just embarrassed. I love my friends, but I wish they would go away."

"We will go to a different place so you can learn without an audience," Kezzie said. "Follow me."

They hopped on the chairlift and went up the hill.

"I can't ski down this big mountain," Gracie said.

"Don't worry. We will take an easy trail," said Kezzie.

They were high above the trees and snow. Gracie saw birds flying and skiers gliding.

She saw a tiny piglet and mother skiing together. The mother was holding on with two long ropes as the little one snowploughed in front.

When it was time to get off the lift, Gracie did just as Kezzie told her. She stood up when Kezzie said, "Now!"

Gracie shuffled her skis and leaned forward.

Then Gracie slid down the exit ramp and toppled straight over.

Kezzie scooped her up and quickly moved her out of the way of the next skiers.

Gracie was angry. She had fallen again. And she certainly didn't like being picked up like a baby. Thank goodness the Sprites couldn't see her now!

A BRILLIANT IDEA

Kezzie unzipped a pocket. She pulled out two ropes attached to a belt.

"No way!" said Gracie. "That's for babies."

"No, it's not," said Kezzie. "It's for beginners."

Gracie crossed her arms and shook her head.

Kezzie sat beside her. "I think you are very brave. It's not easy to learn a new sport. I never could learn to swim."

Gracie gasped. "But it's so easy!"

"Not for me," said Kezzie. "Every time I tried I just sank. My friends always laughed. So I stopped trying."

Gracie looked at the rope and belt Kezzie was holding. She had a brilliant idea!

"I will try again," Gracie said, "if you let me teach you to swim tonight. No one is going to laugh."

Kezzie nodded. "It's a deal."

Gracie did what Kezzie told her. She wore the learning belt. She kept her skis in a V. She made turns by leaning on one ski when Kezzie tugged on that side.

Best of all, with her teacher holding the ropes, she never went too fast.

The Sprites stood and cheered on the balcony when Gracie reached the bottom.

Gracie waved at her friends. Then she said to Kezzie, “Let’s do it again!”

Maybe having her friends there wasn't so bad after all.

That evening in the hotel swimming pool, Kezzie did just as Gracie told her.

Kezzie bobbed, floated and kicked.

They shared a swim noodle and kicked their way up and down the pool.

"This is fun!" said Kezzie.

Then Kezzie and Gracie heard lots of cheers. The Sprites were there to support Gracie and her new friend.

“It is really nice to have friends here for support,” Kezzie said.

“It certainly is,” Gracie said. “And it’s always nice to make a new friend.”

GLOSSARY

balcony platform that sticks out from the outside of a building

chairlift line of bench-like chairs hanging from a moving cable; it carries skiers to the top of a hill or mountain

embarrassed feeling shy or uncomfortable

performance presentation of something entertaining

resort place people go for fun or relaxation

snowplough make a V with skis to slow down or stop

support give strength or comfort to someone

toppled fell forward

TALK ABOUT IT!

1. Do you think it was a good idea for Gracie to try skiing? Why or why not?
2. Do you think Kezzie was a good teacher? Explain your answer.
3. Talk about a time you felt embarrassed. What did you do about it?

WRITE ABOUT IT!

1. Write about a sport or activity you would like to try.
2. Make a list of things Kezzie did to help Gracie learn to ski.
3. Write about a time you tried something new.

About the author

Marsha Qualey is the author of many books for readers young and old. Though she learned to swim when she was very young, she says she has never tried any of the moves and spins Gracie does so well.

Marsha has four grown-up children and two grandchildren. She lives in Wisconsin, USA, with her husband and their two non-swimming cats.

About the illustrator

Kristyna Litten is an award winning children's book illustrator and author. After studying illustration at Edinburgh College of Art, she now lives and works in Yorkshire, with her pet rabbit, Herschel.

Kristyna would not consider herself a very good swimmer as she can only do the breaststroke, but when she was younger, she would do a tumble roll and a handstand in the shallow end of the pool.

Discover more at
www.raintree.co.uk